林鷺 著
Poems by Lin Lu

戴珍妮、黃暖婷 譯
Translated by Jane Deasy,
Faustina Nuanting Huang

忘 秋

Forgetting

Autumn

林鷺漢英雙語詩集
Chinese - English

台灣詩叢 • Taiwan Poetry Series 04

【總序】詩推台灣意象

叢書策劃／李魁賢

　　進入21世紀，台灣詩人更積極走向國際，個人竭盡所能，在詩人朋友熱烈參與支持下，策畫出席過印度、蒙古、古巴、智利、緬甸、孟加拉、馬其頓等國舉辦的國際詩歌節，並編輯《台灣心聲》等多種詩選在各國發行，使台灣詩人心聲透過作品傳佈國際間。接續而來的國際詩歌節邀請愈來愈多，已經有應接不暇的趨向。

　　多年來進行國際詩交流活動最困擾的問題，莫如臨時編輯帶往國外交流的選集，大都應急處理，不但時間緊迫，且選用作品難免會有不週。因此，興起策畫【台灣詩叢】雙語詩系的念頭。若台灣詩人平常就有雙語詩集出版，隨時可以應用，詩作交流與詩人交誼雙管齊下，更具實際成效，對台灣詩的國際交流活動，當更加順利。

　　以【台灣】為名，著眼點當然有鑑於台灣文學在國際間名目不彰，台灣詩人能夠有機會在國際努力開拓空間，非為個人建立知名度，而是為推展台灣意象的整體事功，期待開創台灣文學的長久景象，才能奠定寶貴的歷史意義，台灣文學終必在世界文壇上佔有地位。

　　實際經驗也明顯印證，台灣詩人參與國際詩交流活動，很受

3

重視，帶出去的詩選集也深受歡迎，從近年外國詩人和出版社與本人合作編譯台灣詩選，甚至主動翻譯本人詩集在各國文學雜誌或詩刊發表，進而出版外譯詩集的情況，大為增多，即可充分證明。

承蒙秀威資訊科技公司一本支援詩集出版初衷，慨然接受【台灣詩叢】列入編輯計畫，對台灣詩的國際交流，提供推進力量，希望能有更多各種不同外語的雙語詩集出版，形成進軍國際的集結基地。

2017.02.15誌

目次

3　【總序】詩推台灣意象／李魁賢

9　想念母親・Missing Mother

12　牡羊星圖・The Star Map of Aries

13　兒子當兵・My Son's Military Service

15　詩的天窗・Poetry's Skylight

17　玫瑰・Rose

19　最後一眼・The Last Glance

21　道之門・The Door of Tao

23　一個問題・Una Pregunta

26　給詩人米思特拉爾・To Gabriela Mistra

27　詩在深夜的Ciego de Ávila・
　　Poetry in the Depths of the Night in Ciego de Ávila

29　垂死・Dying

31　給索南措・For Suo Nan Cuo

33　青年Thakur・A Youth Named Thakur

35　在或不在・Absence or Presence

37　面對喜瑪拉雅山脈・Facing the Himalayas

38　銀手鐲・The Silver Bracelet

40　你的歌聲・Your Singing Voice

42　風神・God of the Wind

44　黃昏海岸・The Coast at Dusk

46　海之約・The Pact of the Sea

48　異想之境・The Realm of the Whimsical

49　紫色的風鈴絮語・Rolling Whispers of the Purple Bellflower

50　紅豆情・The Sentiment of the Red Bean

51　秋・Fall

52　我的窗・My Window

53　玫瑰的顏色・Color of the Rose

54　故鄉ê風・Wind in My Hometown

55　風的容顏・Confession to the Wind

57　歸鄉路（一）・The Road back Home (I)

59　歸鄉路（二）・The Road back Home (II)

61　這一頁・This Page

63　傷心夢土・Broken-hearted Land of Dreams

64　旗的私語・Whispers of a Flag

66　鷹的眼罩・An Eagle's Hood

68　王者的天空・The Tyrant's Sky

70　不要隨便跟詩人握手・
　　No Thoughtless Handshaking with a Poet

71　你該流淚・You Ought to Cry

74　霧中樹・Trees in the Mist

75　一朵花・A Flower

76　遺忘吧・Lost in Time

78　曲・Song

79　綺情・Affairs

80　作者簡介 • About the Author

81　譯者簡介 • About the Translators

想念母親

想念母親我心碎裂
一如擊碎海岸的太平洋波濤
那是我擦也擦不乾的眼淚
她的孤單竟舖成一張單薄得
回不了家的床
母親躺在電話線無法抵達的
那一端

想念母親陽光下的慈顏
我來摸摸她日夜愛戀的花草
等待加護病房的門開
告訴她
供桌上的佛祖聞得到花香
她白色的壽衣並沒有黃斑
繡花壽鞋上
已替她縫上兩顆發亮的珍珠

它們的光彩如燈
來日將一路照亮她回歸靈山

想念母親
在吻別她的額頭以後
陪我趕路的太陽也開始疲憊
逐漸沒入
兒時曾經無憂歡笑的海那一邊
想起母親
輕輕碰觸就叫出的聲音
有如針筒
在我的心臟注射她的痛

想念母親的想念
她多麼想回家
即便耗去她一生的老宅
骨架也已如同她一般衰敗

想念母親的寂寞
我變成一座蓄洪的水壩
滿溢的眼淚
在深夜不自覺默默地宣洩

牡羊星圖

廣袤的天空布滿剛強的柔情和堅毅的野心
我曾經迷航在那張上蒼設定好的星圖
妳問我親子為何在人世間別無選擇的相遇

文字的敏感度證實學識的晶片必植入孤獨
可以從漢聲小百科裡自學狗爬式泳技
卻無法掌控一顆球在操場自由滾動的速度

終究已讓自己握住一方被蓄意遺棄的國土
讓郁郁花草默默地植株在自己的土地
那隱藏原生密碼的染色體也正複製著理型

牡羊對自我解釋固執來自性別弱勢的抗衡
我把朝代的對照表布置在書房小天地
想像恁妳依照自己的意象規劃的專屬星圖

兒子當兵

兒子就要去當兵
他擁抱我
說
只不過去參加
一個比夏天還長的夏令營

初嘗
「絕對服從」是鐵的紀律
「不容挑釁」屬於軍中倫理
「荒謬威權」更叫絕對合理

向來樂觀的兒子
安慰自己
當作是一場人生喜劇
學蠶破繭
蛻變成一隻
真正會飛的蛾蝶

不過
昨天深夜
忽然
從刺耳的手機聲中驚醒
匆匆接收一句：
只想聽聽媽媽的聲音

詩的天窗

有一種天窗
只為
虛無的浪漫開啟
星月說
真的很寂寞

有一種天窗
為了度過漫漫長夜
不得不
從心靈的深處開啟
星月說
流淚了
孤寂

望向愛河對岸的詩句：
「痛苦會過去
美麗會留下來」

你為我
開啟一扇
驚喜
我們共同閱讀
詩的天窗
星月說
享受美麗

玫瑰

她是一朵玫瑰
曾經含苞迎接青春盛放的
玫瑰

她是一朵玫瑰
曾經因愛撫而夢想陶醉的
玫瑰

她是一朵玫瑰
曾經艷麗於鼻息親吻的
玫瑰

她是一朵玫瑰
竟然忘記自己滿身利刺的
玫瑰

然而
她是漸次萎謝著的一朵
玫瑰
一朵確實曾經
活過的
人間玫瑰

最後一眼

終於知道
老了也會像小孩子
因為看不到媽媽
就躲起來偷偷哭泣

為了看看媽媽
撐著的傘
一路抵擋強力海風的吹折
為了摸摸媽媽的鼻息
無情的雨
打向我急走而汗濕的衣衫

就在這一天
媽媽努力睜開她的眼睛
看了我
最後的一眼

再也找不到媽媽

暗夜裡
獨自不停偷偷地啜泣
原來我只不過是
一個
老了的小孩

道之門

在眾多走向高點的步伐中
時間已經敗壞
我這世的家人正與我同行
一起在廢墟中
體驗崇高與卑微

有一種存在
連天空都無法盡然俯視
有一種想望
曾經以高塔的堆築
想要和天空對話

所有的奇蹟都無法丈量
所呈現的不可思議
深深隱含
一種不想被摧毀的慾望
然而　看得出
時間還在默默地敗壞

如果恐懼只是繼續停留地面
確實僅能目視到一個門
一個遙遠在天際
虛無著的
空門

仰望清澈的藍天
仰望人間須彌的最高處
隱然存在
一個深不可測的暗示
靠近崇高
靠近美
靠近四方皆在的道之門
我和我這世的親人
在吳哥窟
見識時間以無聲的力量
不止息地敗壞著永恆

一個問題

——to Pablo Neruda

我來
以詩　以歌
以海浪的聲音與味道
造訪你的浪漫

我在你的臥房裡流連
默默感受
愛情存在摧毀一個人的力量
如同窗外的波濤
強烈撞擊你給愛人的一個問題

Una Pregunta

你說
愛情不只是
身體與身體的對話
你說

相愛的人都應該堅定信仰
隱藏在愛情裡的祕密

情人們啊！
當愛情來訪的時候
你們必須傾注相互摧毀的能量
攜手進入靈魂的天堂

我來
站在你的床前
細聲朗讀你寫給愛人的一個
問題的顫動

可歌頌的詩人啊！
你的情詩和著陽光和海浪
正熱烈地

在你明朗又曖昧的臥房窗外
交纏

給詩人米思特拉爾

──to Gabriela Mistral

我聽到小孩們嘻嘻哈哈的笑鬧聲
妳的詩在溜滑梯
妳的詩在盪鞦韆
妳的詩在遠遠的山坳裡翠綠
走向妳的天空清藍無比
我已經品嚐妳的智利
紅酒溫潤而香醇
讓我舌尖上的詩意也醉醺
妳屋前不知名的大樹
以橘橙的髮葉展示妳心中的季節
妳簡單溫馨的臥房廊外
有一朵純白的玫瑰說著妳的話語
妳的詩在小花園徘徊
妳的詩在樹蔭下沈思
妳的詩在妳安息的小山丘上
聆聽並擁抱詩人們獻給妳的心情

詩在深夜的Ciego de Ávila

庭園的夜分外溫柔

詩是語言

詩也不是語言

詩是越境的心情

詩是無國界的愛語

詩在深夜的Ciego de Ávila

大聲呼喚出Taiwán母親的名字

遙遠啊

遙遠的征途

以詩的榮耀說出自己的定位

在同樣有著被殖民傷痕的地方

詩是心靈的慰藉

詩是夜空的流星雨

詩是深夜的馬啼聲

扣囉扣囉

一陣來　一陣去

敲打著詩在夜裡交會的節奏

米黃色的西班牙式建築
溫存了
詩在深夜的Ciego de Ávila

垂死

生長在一片天然野地
你不知名
你無聲無息
你垂下失去活力的頭顱
抵抗著死亡的引力
陽光沒有差別心地照耀著你
海浪卻撞擊著崖石歌唱
鷂鷹悠閒又自負
在寬廣無邊的海上藍天
展翅玩弄著風的流速
遠處的礁石
傳來海獺家族的示威號鳴

我們相遇
在這放眼無人看管的花草叢裡
你不經意地讓我閱讀了
自生自滅的自然律

我用鏡頭永恆了你的不甘心
雖然春天在智利
正熱烈催熟
滿山遍野的動情激素
獨獨你
讓我疼惜
兀自在這裡的掙扎與憔悴

給索南措

綰著一個俐落的髮髻
妳的眼波流動清澈的寂寞
我們伸出手腕
收藏妳為我們祈福的紅絲帶
欠身讓妳為我們披上
如雪的哈達

親愛的索南措啊
妳窗外的山谷
就要開始瀰漫黃昏的薄霧
孩子從幼兒園接回以後
母女又將一起溫習
男主人掛在牆壁上的笑容

我們就要繼續面對
另一段漫長旅途的征戰
離開這沒有魚的世界
懷念從妳的聲音

漂流出的
對於海湖嚮往的信息

妳說你們因為相遇
所以選擇分離
我說我們因為錯過
所以偶然相遇
流浪的雪山獅子旗
用預約希望與幸福的承諾
裝飾妳空白的那面牆壁

親愛的索南措啊
妳說妳對於愛情的承諾
不能回頭
回頭將是一輩子的分離
令人不安的是
必須等待無法計數的雨季

青年Thakur

邊境的旅行開啟了奇妙的機緣
你是我前世的兒子嗎
我們可曾相約在Amritsar相見
短短幾天
熟悉勝過數十年

你說你的專長是咖啡和水煙
我端詳你的眼神
竟然有我生命裡的浪漫
爽朗的笑聲絲毫也沒有雜染
擁著我的肩
牽住我的手
左一聲Mama
右一聲Mama
我們一起走在
沙塵暴來襲的Amritsar街道
黃昏的樹看起來格外蒼老

我怎能不憐惜你
年輕又無比成熟的風霜

你是我前世的兒子嗎
陪我在Amritsar臥病的床榻
離開以後
竟然成為一個母親日夜的牽掛

註：2011年5月下旬我與兒子自助旅行到印度錫克教的勝地阿姆利
澤（Amritsar）並由居住當地的青年Tharkur陪伴到印巴邊界而
結下奇特的因緣。

在或不在

Oh, my dear son
消失了的臉書
因為你不在
或者
其實你一直還在
還在鬱悶的黃昏裡
因為是一個丈夫的緣故
不得不陷入
風沙經常來襲的困頓

活在Amritsar
通往住家巷道的出口
小販們是否依舊
依舊忙著製作各式甜點
好讓生活苦澀的人們
摻入一絲絲
可以暫時遺忘的安慰

而這個世界
在臉書
可以在也可以不在

面對喜瑪拉雅山脈

我終於走向了你
走向你無比寬敞的懷抱裡
你垂掛無數奔流的紗幔
用豪邁的沉靜撞擊我心靈的視窗
我終於豁然明白
純潔的原色來自雪的故鄉

巍峨征服了萬物的卑微
渺小臣服於天地最初的信息
幾株逆風顫危危挺立的小樹
就在不可思議的雪色山巔盡頭
我終於靠近了你
靠近泰戈爾醞釀過的不朽詩篇裡

銀手鐲

魚的圖騰註記著妳的族群
黝黑的膚色
必須以純銀的亮度來打光
雞啼豬鳴的混沌歲月
不怕植物的天然手染暈漬
正好由細針細線
來穿梭時間的細縫
縫縫補補
拼拼貼貼
至於男人山野獵物的不足
魚確實很適合想像

藉著友誼的手
妳費力為我戴上的銀手鐲
我再也不曾拔下
那雙不斷琢磨著我的體溫
復活的魚眼睛

如今卻意外的明亮
日日
在妳無法臆測的浪紋裡騰躍
我只想告訴妳
魚與浪註記著雲煙交會的光彩
手鐲的亮度
已經測試了不會再見的純度

你的歌聲

你的歌聲
呼喊我心中的草原
我心中的草原
在喀喀的馬蹄聲中
頂著藍天白雲
遼闊到無止境的天邊

你的歌聲
呼喊我心中的海洋
我心中的海洋
捲起壯闊的波濤
在我滿溢醇酒的杯中
起伏蕩漾

啊！被海洋激盪拍擊的草原
響起雄壯奔騰的節奏
那是你的歌聲

跳動詩的心臟
流動天籟的音符
化作夜幕中的
點點星光

啊！你的歌聲
顫動馬頭琴美麗的傳說
嘹亮牧民豪邁的
天地蒼涼

風神

我從不認真於祢的形象
在多風的海港
祢曾暴怒
劫走鄰居勇健的漁郎

我從不經意於那一面牆
卻望見祢彷若達摩
飄浪渡海
神情剛席捲過
一片無法估量的草原

我不清楚
星星　月亮　太陽
帶給祢何種神祕的意向
只看到祢轉身的寂寞
掀動雲的衣裳
揚起一位神祇的威嚴

如果我還保留
一丁點
超越凡塵的意念
必是因為與祢相遇
在草原
所以熱切追隨祢
隨意揮灑詩的語言

黃昏海岸

我們等到了黃昏
還是黃昏終於等到了我們
我們總也旅行到
這段綿延著過去的海岸

風雨過後
漂流木的辛酸
上了岸
細說一段又一段
相似卻並不一樣的故事

我們手中咖啡的香醇
從時間的指縫
散溢出
點點浮動的漁船
正從遠方一一點燈歸航

沉默的龜山島
漸漸模糊的地平線
我們終於
沐浴在這片
即將隱沒的黃昏海岸

啊！我們內在的海景
也以無比平靜
去呼應那
起伏青春與愛情的波浪

海之約

被雨滴敲響的日子
我們相約一起去看海
海的蔚藍拒絕造訪
灑上濛濛的灰
提鮮崖坡上
咖啡小屋的藍白色調
我們的笑聲
被那海天象連的
圓弧形地平線擁抱
放牧眼波
漁船在長窗上寫生
飄蕩海的風情
咖啡的香氣移位場景
北海岸的希臘氣息
讓休眠的愛情
呼應起詩的叫喚
不知不覺

從死灰當中甦醒
我們相約一起去看海
在那個
被雨滴敲響的日子裡

異想之境

你想穿透一個夢境
聽一聽風在遠方的處境
她沙啞的嗓音
有時在危高的山崖高歌
有時在幽暗的深谷搜尋
她赤裸的雙腳
長著透明的翼翅
有時向橘色的漠地靠近
有時向雪國的故鄉挑釁
她讓遠方的風帆
看見即將沉沒的夕陽
她讓無趣的戈壁
在黑暗飲酒的夜裡
有了金色的幻夢

紫色的風鈴絮語

淺釋紫色的深度
有了一些些粉紅的竊喜
還是叫我紫色風鈴花吧
當我以一棵樹的姿態出現
卻不留下任何葉片的時候

請允許我身上的花瓣
以最光燦的姿態
返照冬日夕陽的迴光
此刻的巧遇
絕非刻意的誘惑

請記憶我向晚的容貌
在你已懂得黃昏的時刻
微風中
我本是一株
奇幻又浪漫的紫色風鈴木

紅豆情

季節的山丘
懷想
曾經有過的輕狂
手織的香巾
也曾濕透
遠方揮別的柔情

痛徹的心
凝結成粒粒
殷紅的思念
憔悴乾枯的形體
在歲月的更迭當中
剝離
以血的顏色
呼喚不死的愛情

秋

不願
被接收成一顆落果
在春夏的季節漸去漸遠之後
開始思考
熟透了的果香
能拒絕什麼樣的誘惑

想起
一頭脆弱的髮根
忽然同情起
一棵樹
在
秋天
的
心情

我的窗

為了不想囚禁一間房
就開啟一扇窗
窗外
流動著
時間與季節的心情

看一看一天的開始
探一探一天的溫度
測一測一天的可能

我的窗
是一幅變動的風景
有我的沉思
當黃昏
偷偷靠近的時候

玫瑰的顏色

像夜一般的玫瑰的顏色
在冷藏的櫥窗裡
究竟要被拿來送給誰
懷疑她們的品種不夠純淨
或許才能譁眾取寵
對於路過的眼神

掌握著智者般愛的代言權
即使有九十九朵的熱烈
畢竟還有一朵僅存的缺陷
看不到被隱藏的莖刺
在必然需要包裝的年代
玫瑰有了像夜一般的顏色

故鄉ê風

故鄉ê風有海水ê鹹味
六叔公仔做ê風吹嘛捌佇天頂咧飛
聽底咧講
阿公仔　彼冬時
順風坐船到廈門去做生利
阿嬤捌佮子孫講：
咱ê公媽牌毋擱再倒轉去唐山
這是咱世世代代ê故鄉

故鄉ê風有沙佇咧飛
防風林內阮聽到海湧咧講話
漁船ê燈火哪閃爍，天就漸漸黑暗去
厝邊ê阿叔隨風出海去掠魚
煞毋擱再倒轉來團圓

故鄉ê風是我即世人ê好朋友
我ê初戀嘛佇風中發生
伊知影我少年時裤ê眠夢佮心情

風的容顏

——風箏達人的愛戀

捉摸不到的
風的容顏
我該如何向她表白
表白
此生此世的愛戀

啊！風呀風
我愛你
愛你知道天空的寂寞
更愛你
愛你了知消遙的自在

啊！風呀風
我已然耗盡一生
甘心為你
彩繪多彩多姿的容顏

啊！風呀風
我以一根白髮的寬度
伸向天空的遼闊
感知妳的存在
傾訴對你恆長的愛戀

歸鄉路（一）

——記巴拿馬Chepo農場的一位台灣人

乾季一到，火橙刺紫的樹花便出其不意的，沿著幽幽曲曲的碎石子路，肆無忌憚的野放開來。

我問我的寂寞：

怎麼也可以跟著如此喧囂？

艷陽總是無情的炎烤，偶有樹蔭，陪伴的卻是絲掛蠕動的毛毛蟲，而異地成鄉的蟬呀！總是在這季節，忘情的為我演奏自我放逐的哀樂。

我……

逐漸老邁的步伐，

　　緩慢在　漫漫長夜的

歸鄉路

而，你的驚悚

　　卻早已延伸到

　　雨季泥淖的斷橋水涯

而，你的驚喜

　　也早已觸動

　　豎翅汲水的蝶群

引燃一陣
狂亂的飛舞

歸鄉路（二）

——記巴拿馬內地Santiago，
　曾經遭受白色恐怖的異鄉人

塵沙飛揚千萬里
我是蒲公英的種子
隨著風速　載浮載沉
終於　宿命的落腳在
這沙漠荒涼的小村落

而我的惶恐與寂寞
早已習慣的被稱做「Paisano*」
難以被辨識的
古銅黝黑的膚色
是
我不得不被同化的
哀愁

睡夢中
拼死命也無法逃離的是
白色恐怖無限延伸的魔帳

我　只好幻化成
一隻自我截肢的蜥蜴
痛斷綿延數十載的
歸鄉路

*西班牙語「同胞」之意。

這一頁

你翻開這一頁
我翻開這一頁
他翻開這一頁
我們共同翻開的
這一頁

空白
等待無盡的期盼
還是
永遠的告別

暗夜裡
有人
在背棄的曠野裡
哭泣

像白色畫布
被亂刀劃破的
這一頁
是否將變成
風雨中
一枝飆飛的白幡
拍饗
無法回頭的
記憶

傷心夢土

我的夢土流落在黑暗的邊緣
呼喚你的良知
你那可作為的權柄與生命
來自布滿荊棘與試煉的地獄
那兒鮮血曾經流淌
那兒口舌曾被封閉
那兒死神曾經猖狂
那兒靈魂曾經抵抗
還有眾多的心留下缺角
正在永不回頭的歷史裡
等待圓滿
我的夢土蹲在黑暗的角落裡
嚶嚶哭泣
如今
她是一個錐心刺骨的母親
在風霜織就的皺紋裡
起身點起一盞流淚的燈

旗的私語

誰說我是一面旗
啊　啊
請不要把你的意識
隨意投射在我的身上

我既無愛慾
　　也無私情
我既不神聖
　　也不污穢

不要搖我
不要搖我
千萬不要搖醒我的記憶
在這尷尬的時代
那是多麼紊亂與沈重的代價

我流過血的私處
再也無法誕生可貴的新生命

如果
如果你硬要說
我是
我是一面令人稱頌的旗幟
啊　啊
我倒要摀著臉
　　　偷偷地哭泣

因為
因為無論如何
我不想
我不想當一塊
在風雨飄搖中被輕取下來
清洗再掛上的遮羞布

鷹的眼罩

鐵匠精心打造
一隻鷹
對於天空的揣度
以及
牠對於主人的忠誠度

自由向來
不只是單純的想像
雖然
獵殺　未必是
一隻鷹
從高空往下俯視的
唯一慾望

鐵匠鎮日精心打造
一隻鷹
合宜又精緻的面罩

為的是隔絕牠
終日對於天空的愛戀
抑或只是
等待
天空暗下來以後
鷹對於主人的歸順

王者的天空

這是一片無邪的天空
一隻鴿子飛過
一隻烏鴉飛過
一隻琵鷺飛過
一隻最後的春燕
　　　飛過……

這是一片無私的天空
飛來一隻盤旋已久的禿鷹
張開無比巨大的翅膀
乘著氣流
上下左右
掌控一整片天空

被長久爭論不休的
天空　終於失去眾鳥的聲音
被地面仰望的

是一片逃亡的天空
是一片哀傷的天空
是一片王者的天空

不要隨便跟詩人握手

詩人的手是純潔的嗎
詩人的手是柔軟的嗎
詩人的手是浪漫的嗎

土地
人民
熱血
眼淚
無染的真理
不都是詩人用手寫下的隱喻嗎

請不要隨便跟詩人握手

我看到高處的風信雞
指著風向的
竟然是一隻詩人的手

你該流淚

流淚吧
你該流淚的
當敵人站在你的土地上
稱呼你為「鄉親同胞」的時候
你該流下警覺的眼淚

流淚吧
你該流淚的
當你豢養的公僕
正熱切與敵人擁抱的時候
你該留下絕望的眼淚

流淚吧
你該流淚的
當我們手無寸鐵的孩子
築起一道道恐懼的手鍊

猶高喊「和平人權」的時候
你該流下驕傲的眼淚

流淚吧
你該流淚的
當你的母親放下鍋鏟
走向街頭
在人群裡高聲吶喊的時候
你該流下心痛的眼淚

流淚吧
你該流淚的
當你的孩子被迫拿起棒棍
稱你為「暴民」的時候
你該流下懺悔的眼淚

流淚吧
你該流淚的
當先民血跡已乾的土地
開始染上不明鮮血的時候
你該流下決心的眼淚

霧中樹

選擇在這裡生根
選擇在這裡茁壯
成排的
一列
永不屈服的士兵
守護著這塊土地
曲折的道路

有時陽光
有時風雨
有時一如此刻的
寂寞
在迷迷濛濛的
霧靄中
挺立自省的柔情

一朵花

寂寞是一朵花
開在峻峭的高崖上
抖擻風的無情
領受雨的戲謔

緊緊抓住崖壁
豎起傲岸白衣領的
那一朵
原生的寂寞
堅持擎起生命的喇叭
抵抗一波波
襲擊耳鼓的濤浪

遺忘吧

遺忘吧
當我終於成為
一首
告別詩
何必費心典藏
生命向來
只是
時間流裡的沙漏
沒有征服
只能臣服

遺忘吧
遺忘偉大
遺忘微不足道
遺忘隨風而起的
飄零
當葉子掛著季節

一片片
默默地落下
還是
遺忘吧

曲

單調不是唯一的理由
和諧才是最終的目標

弦的序曲
安撫了一切雜音

旋律悠揚起伏的迴旋
你怎能解釋成琴的哀怨

綺情

愛情是窗檯上
攀爬的藤蔓
既相憐又埋怨

根鬚相隨

不甘寂寞的葉片
喜歡悄悄伸出窗外
尋找天空的綺情

作者簡介

　　林鷺現為笠詩社社務委員兼編輯委員、《台灣現代詩選》編選委員，世界詩人組織成員。曾出版詩集《星菊》、《遺忘》。於2005年與2009年赴蒙古參加台蒙詩歌交流、2014年參加在古巴及智利舉行的詩歌節活動。

譯者簡介

　　戴珍妮，生於愛爾蘭，長於台灣，現居溫哥華的中英文譯者，並為加拿大卑詩省翻譯者學會準會員，以及加拿大文學翻譯者協會（位於蒙特婁康考迪亞大學）會員。

　　黃暖婷，台灣大學政治學碩士，現為台灣經濟研究院國際事務處助理研究員。

　　曾任2016年我國APEC領袖代表團成員，以及2013-2015年我國「APEC未來之聲」青年代表團輔導員。

Forgetting Autumn

Missing Mother

Missing mother, my heart shatters and cracks

Like waves from the Pacific Ocean crushing against the coast

Those are tears that I cannot dry even if I tried

Her loneliness has made itself into

A bed so thin that it cannot return home

Mother lies where phone lines cannot reach

On that end

Missing mother's kind face under the sun

I touch the flowers and plants that she loved by day and by night

Waiting for the doors of the intensive care unit to open

To tell her

The Buddha on the altar can smell the fragrance of the flowers

Her white shroud does not in fact have yellow spots

On her embroidered burial shoes

There already are two shiny pearls that have been sewn on for her

Their luster is like a lamp

In future days they will give light on her way to the western paradise

Missing mother

After kissing her goodbye on the forehead

The sun that had hurried with me on my journey has began to grow tired

And has began to gradually fall into

That place by the sea where there was carefree laughter from childhood

Thinking of mother

The voice that would call out if gently touched

Like a syringe

Injecting her pain into my heart

The sense of yearning when missing mother

How she longed to return home

Even if to the old house that consumed her entire life

The framework was waning like she was

The loneliness of missing mother

I have become a dam that stores floodwater

Overflowing tears

Unconsciously, silently draining off in the depths of the night

The Star Map of Aries

The vast sky is abound with staunch tenderness and determined
    ambition
I once drifted from the course of the star map that Heaven set out
You asked me why parents and children have no other choice but to
    meet in this world

The sensitivity of words confirms that loneliness must be implanted
    in the chip of learning
You could learn by yourself how to swim the doggy paddle from the
    Children's Encyclopedia
Yet could not control the speed of a ball freely rolling across the
    playground

It has ultimately allowed oneself to hold onto the side whose land
    has been deliberately abandoned
To let the luscious plants and flowers silently be planted on one's
    own land
The chromosome with the hidden code of protogenesis is also
    replicating forms

Aries self-interprets that stubbornness originates from the
counterbalance of gender disadvantage
I arrange the Comparison Table of Dynasties in the little world of
the study
And imagine an exclusive star map you planned according to your
own imagery

My Son's Military Service

My son is going to serve in the military

With a hug

He said

It's nothing

But to join a summer camp

More than a swealtering season

At his first time

"Absolute obedience" is the iron discipline

"No provocation" is the ethic in the military

"Ridiculous authority" should be totally agreed

My optimistic son

Told himself

It's nothing but a comedy

Just like a cocoon

Should be transformed
To a butterfly really enjoys the wind

However
Yesterday in the dark night
Suddenly
My cellphone rings pierced my dreams
With a hasty sentence
"I want to hear Mama's voices"

Poetry's Skylight

There happens to be a skylight

That solely opens itself

For empty romanticism

The stars and moon say

It is truly lonely

There happens to be a skylight

That in order to pull through the long nights

Cannot but

Open itself from deep within its soul

The stars and the moon say

Cry now

Loneliness

Glancing at the poetry across Love River's bank

"Pain will pass away,

Beauty will remain."

For me

You opened

A surprise

We read together

The skylight of poetry

The stars and the moon say

Embrace the beauty

Rose

She was a rose

A rose who was in her early puberty with expectations

She was a rose

A rose who was fondled and drawn in her illusions

She was a rose

A rose who blossomed in the breath and kisses

She was a rose

A rose who had forgotten her whole body thorns

However

She is a withering rose

A rose

who did live her whole life and legend with soundless paths

The Last Glance

Finally I got to know

That child hidden in my aging body

Weeping in a secret corner

For mourning my mother no longer there

For seeing my mother

My umbrella

Resisted the wind from the sea

roaring all the way

For feeling my mother's breathe

My clothes

Sweated in my trots

Soaked in the relentless rain

It was that day

Slowly, my mother opened up her eyes

忘秋
Forgetting Autumn

To give me her final glance
With her last strength

Mother is no longer there

In the dark night
Alone I weep and weep again
Getting to know that
I'm nothing
But an aging child

The Door of Tao[*]

Among the many steps walking towards the high point
Time has already been corrupted
My family in this life walk with me
Together in ruins
We experience the noble and the humble

There is a form of existence
That even the sky cannot entirely see
There is a kind of longing
That once built a tall tower
To dialogue with the sky

All miracles cannot be measured
The inconceivable that is made present
Deeply implies
A kind of desire that does not want to be destroyed
Yet, it can be seen

That time is quietly being corrupted

If fear is simply to continue remaining on earth

Then indeed one can only see a door

A distant horizon

An empty door

Of nothingness

Lifting my eyes to the clear blue sky

Lifting my eyes to the highest point of Sumeru in the world

There implicitly exists

An unfathomable hint

Close to the noble

Close to the beautiful

Close to the door of tao that is everywhere

In Angkor Wat

My loved ones of this world and I

Experience the ceaseless corruption of eternity

Through the silent force of time

* Tao, also written as 'dao', is a Chinese language character (word) that holds a variety of meanings, such as: method, path, road, principle, truth, reason etc.

Una Pregunta

——to Pablo Neruda

I come

To visit your romance

With poems

With songs

With the aroma and voices

Of ebbs and flows

Stroll in your bedroom

Silently, I feel

As the tides out of your window

In the tides of love

Conceived a destroying force

In a problem

Breaking your lover

Una pregunta

You said

Love is not limited

In the conversations between the bodies

You said

Those who love each other shall confirm their faith

By hiding their individual secrets of love

Lovers!

When love comes to visit you

You should devote your power of mutual destruction

To break and merge into

The heaven of souls

I come

Standing by your bed

Whispering the tremble of the problem

You wrote in a question to your lover

忘秋
Forgetting Autumn

Oh my adorable poet!

In the whispers I feel

Outside of your bright window

Your love poems are catfighting with the sunshine and tides

In the frenzy of flirting shadows

In Pablo Neruda's house, Valparaiso, Chile.
Oct. 11, 2014

To Gabriela Mistral[*]

In the children's chuckles I heard

Your poems are sliding

Your poems are swinging

Your poems are evergreen in the far-away valley

On the way I walk into your Chile

The sky is so blue and clean

The wine is so gentle and tipsy

And the Muse on my tongue is flushing

In front of your house

The unknown big tree

shows your seasons with yellow leaves

At the corridor outside of your bedroom

A white rose is speaking

忘秋

Forgetting Autumn

Your poems

are wandering in your small garden

Pondering under your tree

And on the hill you rest in peace

Your poems

are listening and embracing

those moods from poets' devotions

* The Chilean Nobel laureate in literature.

Poetry in the Depths of the Night in Ciego de Ávila

Nighttime in the garden is exceptionally gentle

Poetry is a language

Poetry is also not a language

Poetry is a feeling of crossing boundaries

Poetry is a borderless language of love

Poetry in the depths of the night in Ciego de Ávila

I loudly call out the name of my mother Taiwan

Oh how faraway

A faraway journey

To tell of one's bearings through the glory of poetry

In the place where there are the same wounds of colonization

Poetry is the consolation of the soul

Poetry is a meteor shower in the night sky

Poetry is clatter of horse's hooves in the depth of the night

Kou lo, kou lo

A bustle coming, a bustle going

Beating the intersecting rhythm of poetry in the night

The beige-colored Spanish-style architecture

Showers tenderness upon

The poetry in the depths of the night in Ciego de Ávila

Dying

Growing in a land of natural wilderness

You are unknown

You are without sound or stir

You hang your head that has lost vitality

Resisting the gravity of death

Sunlight shines upon you without disparity of heart

Yet the waves of the sea crash against the rocks singing

The sparrow hawk is carefree and arrogant

In the boundless vast blue sky above the sea

Spreading its wings to play with the speed of the wind

The faraway reef

Carries the threatening howls of an otter family

We meet

In what at first glance seems to be an unattended flower bush

You inadvertently let me read

The natural laws that emerge of themselves and perish of themselves

I use a lens to immortalize your unwillingness

Even though spring in Chile

Is now warm and near maturity

A mountain-full of estrogen all around

Only and only you

Do I cherish dearly

Struggling and languishing here alone

For Suo Nan Cuo

With a neat bun capped upon your head

Through your gaze flows a clear loneliness

We extend our wrists

And collect the red silk ribbons you have prayed over

Your bow allows you to cover us with

Snow-like hadas*

Oh dear Suo Nan Cuo

The valley outside your window

Is just about to be filled with the thin mist of dusk

Once your child is picked up from kindergarten

Mother and daughter will then together revise

The smile of the man of the house hanging upon the wall

We are about to continue facing

Another chapter in the long journey of our expedition

Leaving this world without fish

While missing the yearning for messages of the seas and lakes

That drifts

In your voice

You say that because you have met

And so you have chosen to separate

I say that because we have missed out

And so we have a chance to encounter each other

The wandering snow lion flag

Uses a promise reserved for hope and happiness

To decorate your blank wall

Oh dear Suo Nan Cuo

You say you cannot turn back upon

The promise of your of love

To turn back would mean a lifetime of separation

What is troubling is that

You must wait through countless rainy seasons

* Hada, a piece of silk used as a greeting gift among the Tibetan and Mongolian peoples.

A Youth Named Thakur

The journey to the border unfolds a marvelous chance of fate

Are you a son from my past life

Perhaps we had set to meet each other in Amritsar

In a short few days

We are more familiar than several decades

You say your expertise lies in coffee and hookah

I scrutinize the expression in your eyes

It unexpectedly holds the romance of my life

Your hearty laugh does not even hold the slightest defilement

Hugging my shoulder

Holding my hand

Calling mama here

And mama there

We walk together

On the sandstorm-struck streets of Amritsar

The trees look exceptionally old in the sunset

How can I not take pity on you
Youthful and immeasurably mature hardships

Are you a son from my past life
Accompanying me while bedridden with illness in Amritsar
After leaving
To my surprise it has become a mother's daily and nightly solicitude

Note:In late May of 2011, I went on a backpacking trip with my son
to India's Sikh area, Amritsar. We were accompanied by a local
youth named Tharkur to the India-Pakistan border, with whom a
unique fate was forged.

Absence or Presence

Oh, my dear son

In back of your inactivated facebook

I can't tell

Your absence or presence

In the always suffocating dawn

Like sandstorms from time to time

The duty of a husband

builds up walls of dust in your life

In Amritsar*

At the exit of the lane you reside

Are the vendors still busy making

The sweets

to give the comforting dewdrops

to those people living in bitterness

However in the kingdom of facebook

This world makes no significance

for its absence or presence

* Amritrsar is a city in the north-western part of India.

Facing the Himalayas

I have finally walked towards you

Walked towards your immeasurably ample embrace

You suspended countless flowing veils

Striking the windows of my soul with bold silence

At last, I suddenly understand

Pure primary colors come from the snow's hometown

Towering majesty has conquered the lowliness of all things

Insignificance has submitted to the first messages of heaven and earth

A few small trees stand trembling against the wind

On the incredible top of the snow-colored peak

I finally have come close to you

Close to the immortal poems that Tagore once conceived

The Silver Bracelet

The fish totem indicates your ethnic group

A dark skin complexion

Must be brightened by the shine of sterling silver

Chaotic years of cocks crowing and pigs squealing

Not afraid to be stained by natural plant dye

It just happens that a thin needle and thin thread

Shuttle the tiny gaps in time back and forth

Stitching and mending

Patching and pasting

As for the men hunting insufficient prey in the mountains

It is indeed very suitable to imagine the fish

By the hand of friendship

With great effort you place a silver bracelet on me

I will never again take it off

That pair of resurrected fish eyes continuously polish and carve my
　　　body temperature

Yet today it shines unexpectedly brightly

Day after day

Prancing through unimaginable waved patterns

I just want to tell you

The fish and waves mark the glory of clouds and mist intersecting

The brightness of the bracelet

Has already measured a purity which we will never see again

Your Singing Voice

Your singing voice
Shouts for the plains of my heart
The plains of my heart
Push the blues and whites of the heights
Into the boundless skies
Amongst the sound of the horse's trotting

Your singing voice
Shouts for the oceans of my heart
The oceans of my heart
Curl up the surging waves
Tossing and turning
In my goblet full of mellow wine

Ah! The plains that are struck by the surging oceans
Arouse majestic and roaring rhythms
It is your voice

忘秋

Forgetting Autumn

The beating poems heart

Liquid, natural musical notes

Become the sparkling star

Of the nights backdrop

Ah! Your singing voice

Trembles the stunning legend of the morin khuur*

While stirring the boldness

Of the nomadic people

* A stringed instrument with a scroll shaped as a horse's head.

God of the Wind

I was never serious about your image
By the windy seaport
You were once violently enraged
And stole our brave and strong fisherman neighbor away

I never gave much thought to that wall
But looked towards as you were Dharma
Drifting crossing the sea
Your godly expression just swept through
An immeasurable grassland

I do not know
What kind of mysterious intent
The stars, the moon, the sun bring to you

I only see the loneliness as you turn around
To lift the clothing of the clouds
To raise the majesty of a deity

If the slightest little bit

Consciousness that transcends the mortal coil

Still remains in me

It must be because of meeting you

On the grassland

Therefore I earnestly follow you

Sprinkling the language of poetry as I please

The Coast at Dusk

We waited upon the dusk
Or has the dusk finally waited upon us
All things considered we have journeyed to
This part of the coast that extends along

After wind and rain
The bitterness of the driftwood
Comes ashore
And narrates in great detail, one after another
Similar but different stories

The aroma of coffee in our hands
Through the crevices in the fingers of time
Exude
Droplets of floating fishing boats
Each having lit their lights and navigating their returns from afar

Silent Guishan Island

The gradually blurry horizon

At last we are

Bathing on this

Coast at dusk that is about to fade away

Ah! Our inner seascape

With incomparable tranquility

Echo the

Ups and downs of the waves of youth and love

The Pact of the Sea

On a day that raindrops strike and sound

We agree to meet and watch the sea

The azure blue of the sea refuses visitors

And sprinkles a misty grey

It lifts and refreshes

The blue and white tones of the coffee hut on the cliff

Our laughter

Is embraced by that arc-shaped horizon

That connects the sea to sky

Our glancing eyes are grazing

Fishing boats sketch upon the long windows

Drifting upon the scenery of the sea

The aroma of coffee shifts the scene

The Grecian atmosphere of the Northern Seashore

Allows slumbering love

To respond to the call of poetry

Unconsciously

Awakening from the dead ash

We agree to meet and watch the sea

On that

Day that raindrops struck and sounded

The Realm of the Whimsical

You want to pass through a realm of dreams

And listen to the plight of the wind in the distance

Her hoarse voice

Is at times singing with a resounding voice off treacherous tall cliffs

And is at times searching in shadowy ravines

Her bare feet

Have transparent wings

At times they draw near to the orange desert

And at times provoke the snowy home country

She makes the faraway sailboat

See the sunset that is about to sink away

She makes the tedious Gobi

In the dark nights of drinking

Have golden dreams

Rolling Whispers of the Purple Bellflower

To simply explain the depth of the color purple

With a tiny dash of pink secret rejoicing

Just call me purple bellflower

When I emerge with the posture of a tree

But never leave any leaves behind

Please allow the petals on my body

With the most glorious posture

To reflect the last radiance of the winter's setting sun

This moment's chance encounter

Is by no means a deliberate temptation

Please remember my appearance towards the evening

In the moment you have understood the dusk

In a gentle breeze

I was a

Fantastic and romantic purple bellflower tree

The Sentiment of the Red Bean

The hills of the season

Yearn for

The frenzied lightheartedness that once was

A hand-woven fragrant towel

Once was soaking wet

Tenderness waved goodbye from afar

A thoroughly pained heart

Condensed into tiny granules

A vibrant red yearning

A haggard and withered body

Over the changing years

Peeling off

With the color of blood

Calling for undying love

Fall

As the spring and summer were gone

Reluctantly

I am transformed to be a ripen fruit

Begin to ponder

How the ripen scent

Can resist the allure of going unknown

Thinking of

My weak hair roots

Suddenly

My empathy arises

to a tree's

mood

in

Fall

My Window

To open a window

For not imprisoning a room

Out of the window

What is flowing

Is the mood of time and seasons

Take a look at

The beginning of a day

Sniff it out

The temperature of a day

Take a measure

Of the possibility of a day

My window

Is a flowing scenery

Filled with my contemplation

As the dusk

Sneaks in

Color of the Rose

Like the night is the color of the rose
Refrigerated inside the shop window
To whom, after all, will it be given
To suspect that their breed is not pure enough
Perhaps only then can one play to the gallery
Of passing looks

Grasping the right to represent love like a wise man
Even if there is the enthusiasm of ninety-nine roses
There is after all the flaw of one rose still remaining
The hidden stem and thorn cannot be seen
In an era where wrapping is inevitably needed
The rose has the color like the night

Wind in My Hometown

Wind in my hometown was saturated with salty savor from the sea

In the windy days uncle's kite was flying in the sky

It is said

In those old days when the wind was blowing

For business Grandpa sailed to Ē-mn̂g* with the wind

And Grandma said that

Taiwan is our hometown for generations

Our ancestors would never ever go back to China

Wind in my hometown was filled with the sand from the beach

In the windbreak forest I heard the tides were whispering in ebbs
    and flows

Once the light on the fishing boats sparked

The sky was going into dark

For fishing Uncle in my neighborhood went to the sea with the wind

But he would never ever go back to home

忘秋

Forgetting Autumn

Wind in my hometown is my dearest friend for life

And my first crush was also happened in the wind

Only the wind knows my dreams and emotions at my prime

* In Mandarin this city is called Xiamen

Confession to the Wind

How should I confess

Confess my lifelong love

As I can't touch

The appearance of wind

Oh wind, wind

I love you

Love you

because you know

The loneliness of sky

Love you

because you know

The ease of free life

Oh wind, wind

To paint your face with colors

I've spent all my life

忘秋

Forgetting Autumn

Oh wind, wind

With the width of a white hair

I stretch out to the wild sky

To sense your existence

To confess

My affection for a whole life

The Road back Home (I)

——In memory of a Taiwanese at Chepo
Farm in Panama

With the dry season's arrival, the tree blossoms with their fiery orange and provocative purple take one by surprise, as they line the somber winding gravel road, indulgently, recklessly opening in their wild way.

I ask my loneliness:

How can you go along with such a din?

The resplendent sun's always a cruel roast, there being only occasional shade, and for company there's the wriggling caterpillars hanging on their threads, and oh the cicadas who've come from afar to make this their home! Unheeding of all emotions, they perform for me the dirge of self-exile in this season.

I...

Take up my strides that are gradually growing old

Slowly in the uninhibited long night

The way back home

But, you thrill

Has long since touched the heart

Erect of wing, drawing water, the butterfly flock

Fires up a spate

Of mad turbulence

The Road back Home (II)

——In memory of a stranger in Santiago
in the Panamanian interior, who had
suffered the white terror

The dust blows up to cover ten thousand miles
I am the dandelion seed
According to wind speed sometimes floating sometimes setting
And last fatally the foot falls there
In that little lonely village in the desert.

And my dread and solitude
Has long since gone by the name of "paisano"
Almost beyond recognition
Skin color of ancient bronze black
Is
I cannot but be assimilated
Pathos

While dreaming

At the risk of life yet inescapable is

The limitless extension of the devil's canopy of the white terror

I can only metamorphose into

A self-amputating lizard

Painfully breaking the thread that extends decades of

The road back home

This Page

You turn to this page

I turn to this page

He turns to this page

The page

That we all turn to

Waits in vain

For an endless expectation

Or

A forever farewell

At the dark night

Someone

Crying

in the forsaken wilderness

As a white painting cloth

torne by daggers

Wether this page

Will become

A flying white flag in the storm

Patting

Those

Irreversible

Memories

Broken-hearted Land of Dreams

My land of dreams is stranded on the edge of darkness

Calling your conscience

That authority and life of yours

Comes from a hell full of thorns and trials

There where fresh blood once flowed

There where mouths have been sealed shut

There where Death was once rampant

There where souls once resisted

And where many hearts left their missing pieces

It is exactly there in a history that can never turn back

One waits for fulfillment

My land of dreams squats in a dark corner

Whimpers and weeps

As for today

She is like a mother stabbed in the heart

In her wrinkles weaved by frost and wind

She stands up to light a crying lamp

Whispers of a Flag

Who said I was a flag?

Ah! Ah!

Please don't so randomly

Project your concepts on me

As I have nor love

Nor any secret affairs

I am nor sacred

Nor unclean

Do not wave me

Do not wave me

Never wave my memories to life

For in this awkward era

How dear a price it would be

The secret places where I have bled
No longer breed precious new life

If
If you insist on saying
I am
I am I flag that stirs admiration and praise
Ah! Ah!
I'll hide my face
      And secretly cry

Because
Because no matter what
I do not wish
I do not wish to become
A rag that is casually torn down

When storms arise

Covering shameful faces

An Eagle's Hood

The blacksmith carefully crafts

An eagle's

Conjecture of the sky

And

Its loyalty to its master

Freedom has always been

Not only pure imagination

Even though

Hunting and killing may not be

An eagle's

Only desire

When gazing down from the heights of the sky

All day long the blacksmith carefully crafts

An eagle's

Fitly and exquisite hood

To isolate it

From its constant love of the sky

Or to just

Wait

For the sky to darken

And the eagle's return to its master

The Tyrant's Sky

This is a naïve sky
A dove passed by
A crow passed by
A spoonbill passed by
And a last swallow
     Passed by...

This is an open sky
A vulture spread its demonic wings
Hovering around with the wind
It seized the whole sky
From the left to the right
From the top to the down

A sky once received many voices
Finally
Lost the sounds of numerous birds

Looked up by the ground

Is a sky in exile

Is a sky in misery

Is a sky captured by the tyrant

No Thoughtless Handshaking with a Poet

Is a poet's hand pure?
Is a poet's hand soft?
Is a poet's hand romantic?

Land
People
Passion
Tears
Immaculate truth
All are metaphors written by poets

Don't shake with a poet with your thoughtless hands

In a distance I see a weathercock
Ironically
The weathercock is a poet's hand
pointing in the same direction
that the wind is blowing

You Ought to Cry

Cry

You ought to cry

When the enemy is standing on your land

When they call you their "brothers"

You ought to cry tears of realization

Cry

You ought to cry

When the civil servants you are fostering

Are locked in a passionate embrace with the enemy

You ought to cry with tears of despair

Cry

You ought to cry

When our defenseless children

Link chains of fear

While shouting slogans of "Peace and Human Rights"
You ought to cry tears of pride

Cry
You ought to cry
When your mother throws down her ladle
And takes to the streets
When she shouts and cries within the crowds
You ought to cry tears of heartache

Cry
You ought to cry
When your children are forced to resort to sticks and clubs
And are labeled "rioters"
You ought to cry tears of repentance

Cry

You ought to cry

When the land where our forefathers blood flowed and dried

Begins to become dyed with an unknown shade of blood

You ought to cry tears of determination

Trees in the Mist

Chose to root here

Chose to grow here

In rows

In lines

Are the irresistible soldiers

Patronizing the stumbling roads

Of this land

Sometimes it rains

Sometimes it shines

Sometimes

In a misty solitude

I feel

A standstill tenderness

A Flower

Loneliness is a flower
That blooms on a high cliff
Bracing the winds heartlessness
Drawing the rains abuse

Tightly clenching to the cliff
While raising its white collar
Its natural solitude
Demands on blowing the horn of life
Stopping wave after wave
Of deafening waves

Lost in Time

Let it lost in time

When I finally become

A requiem

Let the notes of life

lost in time

Like sands through the hourglass

So are the days of our lives

There people can never conquer the time

But only time can conquer the people

Let everything lost in time

Greatness

Insignificance

Are all leaves on the trees of life

When the season comes

Silently

Leaves are lost in time

So

Let it lost

Let it lost in time

Song

Monotony is not the sole reason

Harmony is the real ultimate goal

The overture of the strings

Appeases all of the noise

The melody circles in gentle flows, rising and falling

How can you interpret this as the sorrow of the qin*

* A fretless Chinese board zither with seven strings.

Affairs

Love is the vine

Twining on the windowsill

Mingled with empathy and grumbles

Bounded, lingered yet reluctant

The leaves like silently escaping

　from the window

To seek the affairs in the sky

About the Author

Lin Lu (b.1955) concurrently serves at the standing committee of the Li Poetry Society, the editorial board of the *"Li Poetry Magazine"*, and the jury of annual Taiwan Modern Poetry Collection. She is also a member of Movimiento Poetas del Mundo (PPdM). Lin Lu's poetry collections are *"Star Chrysanthemum"* and *"Lost in Time"*. She participated Taiwan-Mongolia Poetry Festival held in Mongolia at the year 2005 and 2009, and the poetry festivals held in Cuba and Chile in 2014.

About the Translators

Jane Deasy is an Irish-born, Taiwan-raised, Vancouver-based Mandarin Chinese Translator and Interpreter.

She is an Associate Member of The Society of Translators and Interpreters of British Columbia and a Member of the Literary Translators' Association of Canada (Concordia University, Montreal).

Faustina Nuanting Huang is an assistant research fellow at the department of international affairs, Taiwan Institute of Economic Research. She holds a MA in political science from National Taiwan University.

She was a member of the Chinese Taipei APEC Leader's Delegation in 2016 and the educator of Chinese Taipei APEC Voices of the Future Delegation from 2013 to 2015.

CONTENTS

85   Missing Mother · 想念母親

88   The Star Map of Aries · 牡羊星圖

90   My Son's Military Service · 兒子當兵

92   Poetry's Skylight · 詩的天窗

94   Rose · 玫瑰

95   The Last Glance · 最後一眼

97   The Door of Tao · 道之門

100 Una Pregunta · 一個問題

103 To Gabriela Mistral · 給詩人米思特拉爾

105 Poetry in the Depths of the Night in Ciego de Ávila ·
     詩在深夜的Ciego de Ávila

107 Dying · 垂死

109 For Suo Nan Cuo · 給索南措

112 A Youth Named Thakur · 青年Thakur

114 Absence or Presence · 在或不在

116 Facing the Himalayas · 面對喜瑪拉雅山脈

117 The Silver Bracelet · 銀手鐲

119 Your Singing Voice · 你的歌聲

121 God of the Wind · 風神

123 The Coast at Dusk · 黃昏海岸

125 The Pact of the Sea · 海之約

127 The Realm of the Whimsical · 異想之境

128 Rolling Whispers of the Purple Bellflower · 紫色的風鈴絮語

目次
CONTENTS

129 The Sentiment of the Red Bean · 紅豆情

130 Fall · 秋

131 My Window · 我的窗

132 Color of the Rose · 玫瑰的顏色

133 Wind in My Hometown · 故鄉ê風

135 Confession to the Wind · 風的容顏

137 The Road back Home (I) · 歸鄉路（一）

139 The Road back Home (II) · 歸鄉路（二）

141 This Page · 這一頁

143 Broken-hearted Land of Dreams · 傷心夢土

144 Whispers of a Flag · 旗的私語

147 An Eagle's Hood · 鷹的眼罩

149 The Tyrant's Sky · 王者的天空

151 No Thoughtless Handshaking with a Poet ·
     不要隨便跟詩人握手

152 You Ought to Cry · 你該流淚

155 Trees in the Mist · 霧中樹

156 A Flower · 一朵花

157 Lost in Time · 遺忘吧

159 Song · 曲

160 Affairs · 綺情

161 About the Author · 作者簡介

162 About the Translators · 譯者簡介

語言文學類　PG1758　台灣詩叢04

忘秋 Forgetting Autumn
——林鷺漢英雙語詩集

作　　　者/林鷺（Lin Lu）
譯　　　者/戴珍妮（Jane Deasy）、黃暖婷（Faustina Nuanting Huang）
叢書策劃/李魁賢（Lee Kuei-shien）
責任編輯/林昕平
圖文排版/周妤靜
封面設計/葉力安

發 行 人/宋政坤
法律顧問/毛國樑　律師
出版發行/秀威資訊科技股份有限公司
　　　　　114台北市內湖區瑞光路76巷65號1樓
　　　　　電話：+886-2-2796-3638　傳真：+886-2-2796-1377
　　　　　http://www.showwe.com.tw
劃撥帳號/19563868　戶名：秀威資訊科技股份有限公司
　　　　　讀者服務信箱：service@showwe.com.tw
展售門市/國家書店（松江門市）
　　　　　104台北市中山區松江路209號1樓
　　　　　電話：+886-2-2518-0207　傳真：+886-2-2518-0778
網路訂購/秀威網路書店：http://www.bodbooks.com.tw
　　　　　國家網路書店：http://www.govbooks.com.tw

2017年5月　BOD一版
定價：210元
版權所有　翻印必究
本書如有缺頁、破損或裝訂錯誤，請寄回更換

國家圖書館出版品預行編目

忘秋 Forgetting Autumn : 林鷺漢英雙語詩集 / 林
鷺著 ; 戴珍妮, 黃暖婷譯. -- 一版. -- 臺北市 :
秀威資訊科技, 2017.05
　　面 ;　　公分. -- (語言文學類)(臺灣詩叢 ; 4)
BOD版
ISBN 978-986-326-420-0(平裝)

851.486　　　　　　　　　　106004023

讀者回函卡

感謝您購買本書，為提升服務品質，請填妥以下資料，將讀者回函卡直接寄回或傳真本公司，收到您的寶貴意見後，我們會收藏記錄及檢討，謝謝！
如您需要了解本公司最新出版書目、購書優惠或企劃活動，歡迎您上網查詢或下載相關資料：http:// www.showwe.com.tw

您購買的書名：_____

出生日期：_____年_____月_____日

學歷：□高中 (含) 以下　　□大專　　□研究所 (含) 以上

職業：□製造業　□金融業　□資訊業　□軍警　□傳播業　□自由業
　　　□服務業　□公務員　□教職　　□學生　□家管　□其它_____

購書地點：□網路書店　□實體書店　□書展　□郵購　□贈閱　□其他

您從何得知本書的消息？

　□網路書店　□實體書店　□網路搜尋　□電子報　□書訊　□雜誌
　□傳播媒體　□親友推薦　□網站推薦　□部落格　□其他_____

您對本書的評價：(請填代號　1.非常滿意　2.滿意　3.尚可　4.再改進)

　封面設計____　版面編排____　內容____　文／譯筆____　價格____

讀完書後您覺得：

　□很有收穫　□有收穫　□收穫不多　□沒收穫

對我們的建議：_____

_____

_____

_____

11466
台北市內湖區瑞光路 76 巷 65 號 1 樓

秀威資訊科技股份有限公司　　　收

BOD 數位出版事業部

....

（請沿線對折寄回，謝謝！）

姓　　名：_____　年齡：_____　性別：□女　□男

郵遞區號：□□□□□

地　　址：_____

聯絡電話：(日)_____　(夜)_____

E-mail：_____